MOJANG

MINECRAFT
WOODSWORD CHRONICLES

LAST BLOCK STANDING!

© 2021 Mojang Synergies AB. All Rights Reserved. Minecraft and the Minecraft logo are trademarks of the Microsoft group of companies.

Published in the United States by Random House Children's Books, a division of Penguin Random House LLC, 1745 Broadway, New York, NY 10019, and in Canada by Penguin Random House Canada Limited, Toronto. Random House and the colophon are registered trademarks of Penguin Random House LLC.

rhcbooks.com
minecraft.net

Library of Congress Cataloging-in-Publication Data is available upon request.
ISBN 978-1-9848-5069-0 (trade) |
ISBN 978-1-9848-5070-6 (library binding) — ISBN 978-1-9848-5071-3 (ebook)

Cover design by Diane Choi

Printed in the United States of America
10 9 8 7 6 5

MOJANG
MINECRAFT
WOODSWORD CHRONICLES

LAST BLOCK STANDING!

By Nick Eliopulos
Cover illustrated by Luke Flowers
Interior illustrated by Chris Hill

Random House 🏠 New York

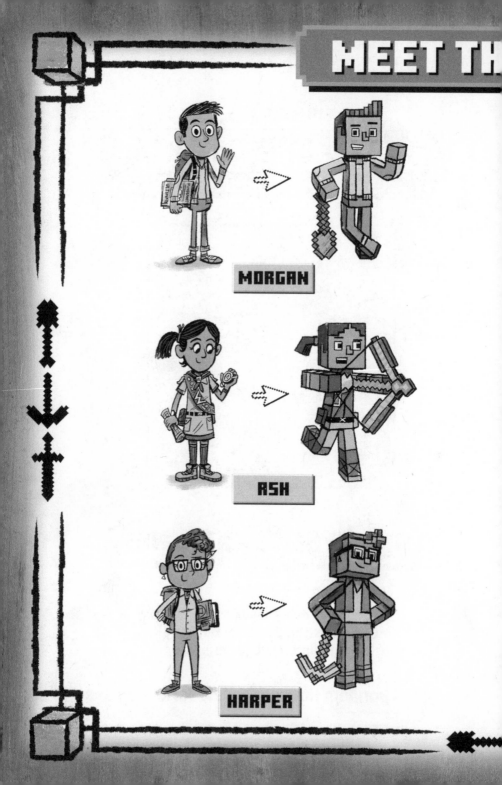

MORGAN

ASH

HARPER

PO

JODI

MS. MINERVA

DOC CULPEPPER

Prologue

DON'T HOLD YOUR BREATH FOR A HAPPY ENDING

Six figures stood in the shadow of a great tower. Inside that tower, high above them, was their enemy. **He called himself the Evoker King,** and he had the power to destroy the game they all loved.

The first figure was determined to stop him. "This is it," she said. **"THE FINAL BATTLE."**

The second figure nodded in agreement. "We're ready," he said.

The third figure looked up at the tower, and his head spun. "Speak for yourself."

The fourth figure put a hand on his shoulder. **"WE'RE WITH YOU ALL THE WAY,"** she promised.

The fifth figure pointed her sword at their new companion. "Are *you* ready?" she asked.

The sixth figure trembled. **It wasn't easy being the new kid on the team.**

But their whole plan relied on him. So he put on a brave face.

"Sure," he said. **"LET'S TAKE BACK MINECRAFT AND BUILD A BETTER WORLD."**

Chapter 1

THE BEGINNING
OF THE END
(AND I'M NOT GONNA CRY!)

Ash Kapoor stepped out of the darkness and into the light of day.

For a moment, she expected the sunlight to dazzle her eyes and warm her skin. But the sun was artificial, and its light didn't make her feel any warmer. The trees were artificial, too, and the grass, and the river running nearby. It was all virtual. *Digital.* **A video game version of reality.**

Here, even Ash's body was an *avatar.* It looked like her, but it was *boxy,* as if constructed using building blocks. **Ash looked at her cube hands and knew they were not made**

out of skin or bone or living cells, but out of millions of tiny bits of light and color called *pixels.* **Her real, flesh-and-blood body was sitting in her school's computer lab.** So were the real bodies of her friends Morgan, Jodi, Harper, and Po.

She looked at her friends' avatars now. **They had just finished fighting their way through a difficult dungeon.** She could sense that they were all tired and a little cranky, but she couldn't tell that by looking at them. **Avatars didn't get dirty or battle-damaged.** They didn't get bloodshot eyes or messy hair. They always looked the same, unless you chose a new "skin" to change your appearance.

They had all used different skins during their dungeon delve so that they would look like fantasy heroes. **But they were back to normal now. They no longer looked like mythic heroes.** They just looked like a bunch of kids.

Well, all of them except Po Chen. As the team's unofficial goofball, he had decided to keep wearing his dungeon skin. **He looked like a wise old wizard.**

"That was *epic*," Po said, not sounding very wizard-like at all.

"It was a disaster," said Morgan Mercado. "We failed. **THE EVOKER KING HAS THE FOUNDATION STONE!**"

Morgan's little sister, Jodi, shrugged. "We don't even know what the Foundation Stone does. Maybe everything will be okay?"

Harper Houston shook her head. "Didn't you

hear the way the Evoker King gloated? And that wicked laugh?" **She shuddered.** "Nobody who laughs like that is up to anything good."

Ash thought Harper was right. Part of her wanted to find the Evoker King immediately. Whatever he was up to, they could still stop him. Maybe.

But they'd all been through a lot. **They needed to rest and heal. They needed**

to restock their supplies and repair their weapons. And they all had homework waiting for them back in the real world!

She was just about to suggest disconnecting for the day . . . when she saw something strange out of the corner of her eye.

In the distance, **the landscape was shimmering.** Far-off blocks seemed to be blinking out of existence and reappearing as quickly as they had vanished. At first it was only the blocks at the far horizon, but as she watched, the strange effect moved toward them like a wave.

"Does anybody else see that?" she asked.

"I've never seen anything like it," said Morgan. "But it's coming this way."

"BRACE YOURSELVES!" Ash said as the blocks all around them flickered. She saw her avatar arms pixelate, and her friends winked briefly out of existence.

It only lasted a moment. The rippling wave moved into the far distance, and **everything looked just as it had before.**

"What in the world was that . . . ?" Ash said.

"Some kind of glitch?"

Harper frowned. **"THE LAST TIME WE CALLED SOMETHING 'JUST A GLITCH,' IT WAS THE EVOKER KING HACKING OUR ENTIRE SCHOOL."**

"You don't think that was him, do you?" Morgan asked. "Did he already do something with the Foundation Stone?"

"WE NEED MORE INFORMATION ABOUT WHAT THE STONE IS," Ash said. "Otherwise, we're just making wild guesses."

"Huh," Po said. "That's weird. . . ."

Jodi turned to him with concern. "What's wrong?"

"I was gonna change my skin real quick," he said. "But it's not working."

Harper put her hand to her chin. "Curious. **THE ANOMALIES ARE MULTIPLYING. . . ."**

"Maybe we should set up our beds and disconnect," said Ash. "It's got to be getting late, anyway. We'll regroup tomorrow."

Morgan seemed uncertain. He looked

to the horizon, in the direction that strange wave had come from.

"Don't worry," Ash said. **"WE'LL FIND HIM. WE'LL STOP HIM."** She put a blocky hand on his shoulder. **"TOMORROW."**

Ash waved goodbye to her friends on the school lawn, then rode her bike the short distance home. The air was crisp, and she smiled at the feeling of real sunlight on her face.

She had only been living in the area for a little while, but Jodi, Morgan, Po, and Harper had all helped her feel like she

belonged here. **She'd also joined the local chapter of the Wildling Scouts,** co-built a bat sanctuary, and stage-managed a school play!

Ash realized she didn't feel like "the new kid" anymore. She had really made a home for herself here.

As she pulled up to her family's house, Ash was

surprised to see her mother's car in the driveway. Her mom often worked late. **Most nights, Ash and her father cooked dinner together,** and her mom took care of the dishes.

When Ash walked through her front door, both her parents were there. It looked like they'd been waiting for her.

"Hello, Ash," said her dad. **"I've baked you a cake."**

"Why don't you have a seat?" said her mom. "We have some good news."

"Great news," said her dad a bit too quickly and too enthusiastically.

Ash thought their smiles looked a little forced. **Whatever news they had for her . . . she thought it probably wasn't good news at all.**

Chapter 2

DON'T FORGET TO STOP AND SMELL THE RAINBOWS! (THOUGH YOU MIGHT NEED TO BRING A STEPLADDER.)

The next morning, **Morgan awoke feeling anxious.** There were too many unanswered questions about what he and his friends would face the next time they put on their VR headsets.

Morgan's science teacher, **Doc Culpepper,** had invented those headsets, and she had asked Morgan and his friends to test them. She seemed to have mostly forgotten about them since then. Doc liked to hop from one project to the next. **For an adult, her attention span seemed awfully short.**

The kids had told Doc that her headsets were amazing, which

was true. Through some advanced science that even Harper didn't understand, **the goggles seemed to transport their minds to another world.** A world that looked and acted almost exactly like Minecraft.

But Morgan and his friends had soon realized they weren't alone in that virtual world. They shared it with a menacing being known as the Evoker King . . . **and a helpful entity who called herself the Librarian.**

The kids had decided not to share those particular details with Doc. The last thing they wanted was for her to take the headsets away to dissect them.

On their walk to school, Jodi quickly picked up on Morgan's mood. **"What's eating you today, big brother?"** she asked.

Morgan sighed. "I'm just going over everything in my head. We never found Doc's missing sixth headset, you know. . . ."

"And you thought that whoever had the headset was secretly the Evoker King."

"But the Evoker King turned out to be

an artificial intelligence," Morgan said. "He's one hundred percent digital. It's the Librarian who has the headset . . . and a secret identity."

"Do you have a theory about who she might be?" Jodi asked.

"I don't," he admitted. "But she obviously knows more than she's told us. If we can find her, she might be able to tell us what the Evoker King is really up to. **Or what the Foundation Stone does."**

"In the past, the Librarian has always found *us,*" Jodi reminded him. "Not the other way around."

"Maybe that needs to change," said Morgan.

By now, the siblings had arrived at the front lawn of the school. **Morgan saw Harper and Po, but Ash wasn't there.** That was unusual. Ash was often the first to arrive.

"Where's Ash?" he asked. "We need to make a plan."

"Haven't seen her," Harper said. Po shrugged.

Jodi peered down the sidewalk. "I'm sure she'll be here soon," she said.

But Ash never showed up on the lawn. Morgan couldn't find her at her locker, either. **She slipped into homeroom mere seconds before the late bell rang.** She gave him a little wave, and Morgan noticed she had dark circles under her eyes. It looked as if she hadn't gotten any sleep.

He wanted to ask her about that. But **Ms. Minerva,** their homeroom teacher, had already started taking attendance, and talking wasn't allowed during attendance.

Apparently, no one had ever mentioned that rule to Doc. The science teacher burst into the classroom in a fit of excitement. **"Class!"** she said. **"Look! Look outside the window!"**

Morgan turned his head in the direction she was pointing. It was easy to understand why Doc was so excited. Stretching across the sky was the most magnificent rainbow Morgan had ever seen.

He'd seen small rainbows before. But this one looked like a drawing out of a storybook. It seemed to spring from the trees and spread through the blue above before arcing back down to the ground. **He could clearly make out each color, from red to violet.**

The whole class oohed and aahed, Morgan loudest of all.

"Can anyone tell me what causes a rainbow to appear?" Doc asked.

Morgan didn't know the answer, but others did. Several students raised their hands. Jodi cried out, **"Leprechauns!"**

Before Doc could call on anyone to answer, Ms. Minerva cleared her throat. Loudly. She glared at Doc over her glasses.

"Excuse me, Doc," said Ms. Minerva. "But this isn't your classroom. It's mine."

"Oh, nonsense," said Doc. **"The world is our classroom, Minerva!** And we have to provide lessons whenever and wherever the opportunity arises. We have to be *flexible*."

"Sounds a bit chaotic," Ms. Minerva replied. She tapped her attendance log. "And it's irresponsible to get distracted before taking attendance."

"A little chaos can be good," said Doc. "If you're too obsessed with rules, you can sometimes miss out on important opportunities."

To make her point, Doc pointed again to the classroom window. Morgan gasped. In the time that the teachers had spent talking, **the rainbow had disappeared.**

"Too bad," said Doc. "We missed our chance."

"That's a pity," said Ms. Minerva. "But, Doc, who's watching your homeroom right now?"

"Oh, they're busy taking care of the frogs," answered Doc.

Ms. Minerva tapped her chin. "Isn't this the same class that let the frogs loose the last time you left them alone? If I recall, we were finding frogs in desk drawers and wastebaskets for weeks. . . ."

Doc's eyes went wide. "Oh no!" she moaned. Doc hurled herself out the door and whipped around the corner at full speed.

Ms. Minerva smirked and returned to making her attendance log.

"Well, that was very exciting, but let's all settle down," she said.

Morgan could tell that she thought she'd won the disagreement. But he wasn't so sure.

And he still didn't know where rainbows came from.

Throughout homeroom, Morgan's eyes kept drifting back to the window. **The rainbow never came back.** But thinking about it did take his mind off the Evoker King for a while.

The bell rang, and Morgan sprang from his seat. It was his day to feed the class hamster, Baron Sweetcheeks. **He loved the hamster,** and always snuck him a few extra pellets.

While he prepared the bowl of food, Ash approached. **She picked up the hamster and nuzzled him.** He chirped happily.

"Morgan, we need to talk," she said.

"I was just about to say the same thing to you!" he said. "I was looking for you this morning. The Evoker King—"

"The Evoker King will have to wait," she said. **"I've got bad news,** and if I don't tell you right now, I'm just going to burst into tears and not be able to say anything at all."

That got Morgan's attention. He put down the hamster food and looked at Ash. Her eyes were wet.

"Ash, what is it?" he asked.

She took a deep breath before answering. "It's my parents. Yesterday they told me . . . they said . . ."

"What?" said Morgan.

"We're moving," said Ash. **"Morgan, I'm leaving Woodsword. Forever."**

Chapter 3

SOMETHING IS ROTTEN IN THE STATE OF MINECRAFT....

Po wondered if his wizard face showed just how upset he was. Maybe the beard hid his frown? **He didn't get angry very often.** Usually, he tried to laugh about stuff that bothered him. But today, he was angry. "I don't understand

how your parents could *do* this to you," he said.

Ash's avatar just shrugged. "It wasn't really their decision. MY MOM'S JOB MAKES HER MOVE SOMETIMES."

"Could she get another job?" asked Harper.

"Could she do her job remotely?" asked Jodi. **"EVERYTHING IS VIRTUAL THESE DAYS!"**

Despite his anger, Po chuckled at that. Everything certainly *was* virtual, where they were standing.

"My mom's definitely not going to get another job," Ash said. "And she has to work on-site, but she *likes* that. She's an engineer. It's her dream job."

Ash had broken the news to them throughout the day, one at a time. They had decided to have a group meeting to discuss it . . . **and to have their meeting in Minecraft, where they had some privacy. The group also had important work to do.**

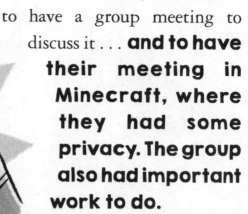

"Now, who has the wither skeleton skulls?" Ash asked.

"Ha!" said Po. "That's one way to change the subject."

"I'VE GOT THE SKULLS," Harper said. "I picked them up along with lots of soul sand and other items when we were in the Nether. You never know when soul sand is going to come in handy."

"We only need three," said Morgan. "You'll need to place them in a row on top of the soul sand."

"But not until we're ready!" Ash said. "We're in for a real battle here."

"IT'S A VERY STRANGE PLAN," said Jodi. "Are we really creating a monster that's going to try to destroy us?"

"Well . . . yeah," said Morgan. "When you put it that way, it's a weird plan."

"We need to talk to the Librarian," Ash said. "And I think building a beacon is the best way to get her attention."

"AND TO MAKE A BEACON, WE NEED A NETHER STAR," said Morgan.

"**AND THE ONLY WAY TO GET A NETHER STAR IS BY DEFEATING A WITHER,**" said Ash.

"And a wither is . . . what, again?" asked Jodi.

Morgan looked sheepish. "**IT'S A SUPER-HOSTILE, FLYING UNDEAD BOSS MOB WITH THREE SKELETAL HEADS.**"

"Oh, good. I was worried it was going to be something bad," Jodi replied sarcastically. "Perhaps we should invite it over for dinner."

"We can handle it," Ash insisted. "**EVERYBODY GET YOUR WEAPONS READY.** Harper, go ahead."

Po held his breath. He watched as Harper placed three pitch-black skulls in a row. Then she took a big step back and drew her sword.

Nothing happened.

"**IT'S NOT WORKING,**" Morgan said.

"Typical!" said Po. "The one time you *want* to face a hostile mob, it doesn't happen."

Ash poked at one of the skulls. Morgan kicked at the soul sand.

Po had a sinking feeling. He *still* couldn't change his avatar skin. He hadn't mentioned it to the others, because it seemed like a minor problem in comparison to everything else they were dealing with. But now he wondered: broken wither, broken skin library. **Was it a coincidence?**

He pulled an ax from his inventory. He took a swing at a nearby tree.

Again: nothing happened.

Once, when Po had been new to the game, he'd tried to cut his way into a mountain using a wooden pickaxe. It had taken *forever* to even make a dent. **Back then, he hadn't known that you were supposed to use a stronger tool to cut through stone.**

He swung again and again, but if the ax was doing anything, he couldn't tell. And this was a diamond ax that he was using. It should have cut through pretty much anything. It should certainly have been able to chop through a tree!

He tried several more times to be sure. **Still nothing.**

"Uh, you guys?" he said. "Am I doing this the right way?"

"That's strange," said Harper. **She pulled an iron shovel from her own inventory.** She tried to use it to dig into the ground, but the shovel was useless. "I don't understand this."

"Let me try," said Jodi. **She pulled out a**

diamond pickaxe and swung it at a rocky hill. The pickaxe bounced off the rock without making a mark.

In the dungeon, Po had seen that pickaxe break through obsidian. Now it couldn't handle a little bit of basic cobblestone?

Something was very wrong here, Po thought.

"Something is very wrong here," said Morgan outloud.

"That's exactly what I was just thinking!" said Po, looking at his friend.

Ash looked stunned. "That energy wave yesterday," she said. **"WHAT IF THAT DID SOMETHING TO THE GAME?"**

Morgan stared at his beloved fancy diamond sword. "Do you think the Evoker King

made it so our weapons and tools don't work?"

"I think it's worse than that," Ash said. Her eyes drifted to the inactive wither with its three silent heads.

"He broke the game," Po sputtered. **"HE BROKE MINECRAFT!"**

And as soon as he'd said the words, he knew they were true.

Chapter 4

IT'S STILL MINECRAFT!
JUST WITHOUT THE MINING.
OR THE CRAFTING.
WHO ARE WE KIDDING?
IT'S BROKEN.

Harper didn't like this one bit. It was as if the Evoker King had locked everything in place. **"IT'S ALMOST LIKE HE FROZE THE GAME,"** she said. "I've never heard of anything like this!"

"I have. Sort of," said Morgan.

Harper tried to pick up one of the wither skulls. But now that she'd put it down, it felt glued in place. "I'm all ears," she said.

"I used to hang out with a guy named Dante," Morgan said. **"HE'S ACTUALLY THE ONE WHO FIRST SHOWED ME MINECRAFT."**

"I remember him," said Jodi, taking another useless swing with her pickaxe. "He was nice!"

"Yeah," said Morgan. "And he was an incredible builder. He liked to re-create famous buildings in Minecraft. He made the Empire State Building, the Shanghai Tower, the Shard . . . you name it."

Harper felt a sudden chill. It had to be her imagination, since they didn't actually get hot or cold here. But she couldn't shake the feeling that the Evoker King was watching them.

Then the sky rumbled with thunder, and she shuddered. **Rain was coming.** It wouldn't hurt them, but it would make everything feel a little creepier.

"Let's walk while we talk, Morgan," she suggested. "Our old starter castle is nearby, remember? We can head that way."

"WHAT ABOUT THE WITHER?" asked Po.

Harper shrugged. "It's not going anywhere."

"Neither are our beds, unfortunately," said Ash. Her ax bounced harmlessly off her bed. "They're stuck, too."

"WE HAVE BACKUP BEDS AT THE CASTLE!" said Jodi. "Remember? We each had our own bedroom set up. Mine was *very* pink."

"So was mine!" Po said happily.

"It's as good a plan as any," said Morgan. "And maybe the Librarian will find us there, since the beacon idea is a bust."

Morgan pulled the compass they had constructed during an earlier adventure from his inventory. He held it out for everyone to see, but the needle stayed in place.

"It's useless," he said.

They all looked automatically to Ash, who had the best sense of direction. At least the sun

still seemed to be moving in the sky, so Ash used it to get her bearings. She pointed over Jodi's head. **"IT'S THAT WAY."**

As they headed in the direction Ash had indicated, Harper said, "Morgan, you were telling us about Dante?"

"Right," Morgan grumbled as he returned the compass to his inventory. "So one day after school, **DANTE SENT ME A MESSAGE AND ASKED ME TO SIGN IN TO HIS GAME SO I COULD SEE HIS LATEST CREATION.** I was expecting something familiar, like the Chrysler Building. But this time, he'd created something totally new! He'd designed his *own* skyscraper for the first time. It was super tall, with tons of glass and these awesome gargoyles. **WE WERE IN CREATIVE MODE,** so I was able to fly up and see all the details."

Harper closed her eyes and tried to imagine what sort of structure she'd make if she had time to build anything. Lately, all their game time had involved life-and-death struggles. **It would be nice just to build again!**

"When I was flying," Morgan continued, "I noticed that one of the gargoyles didn't match the others. **IT HAD A GRAVEL BRICK WHERE A COBBLESTONE BRICK SHOULD HAVE BEEN.** An easy mistake to make, and just as easy to fix! So I took out my pickaxe and tried to remove the gravel. And guess what?"

"You couldn't do it," Harper guessed.

"Right," said Morgan. **"I SWUNG MY PICKAXE, AND NOTHING HAPPENED!"**

"Sounds familiar," Jodi said glumly.

"I asked Dante what had happened," said Morgan. "And he explained that he'd changed the game's settings so that only *he* could 'edit' blocks. In other words, I couldn't take anything apart or *change* anything. Because I was playing on his server, that was something he had control over."

"BUT WHY?" asked Po.

"To protect his creation, of course," said Jodi. **"HE HAD CREATED A GREAT WORK OF ART!**

He didn't want anyone else coming in and putting TNT on it."

"Like a museum," said Harper. "Or my grandma's house. Look, but don't touch."

"Exactly," said Morgan. "It was just like what's happening to us now. **WHICH AT LEAST GIVES US A CLUE AS TO WHAT THE EVOKER KING IS DOING.** I think the Foundation Stone gives him ownership of the server, so to speak. It gives him the power to decide who can edit blocks. At least we can still *place* blocks, for now, but that doesn't leave us with many options."

"We're here," said Ash, and Harper looked past the next hill. **There stood their castle**—or what was left of it. It had definitely seen better days.

It was raining now, and the gloomy weather made the castle look a little sinister. **Haunted.** But it would be safer than being out in the open.

She hoped so, anyway. But she still couldn't shake the feeling that they were being watched.

"Oh, look!" Jodi cried. "Over there. **IT'S A HORSEY!**"

Harper looked where Jodi was pointing. There was a horse standing near the entrance of the castle. It raised its head to look at them. . . .

Just then, a bolt of lightning lit up the sky. It illuminated the horse, revealing it to be a hideous skeleton! It was nothing but white bone and black hooves. Harper could see right through its rib cage!

Jodi screamed.

Lighting flashed again. This time it struck the horse. Harper gaped. She

had never seen anything struck by lightning! She stepped forward to see if the horse was injured. She wanted to help it if she could—even if it was a monstrous mob!

But the lightning had done worse than hurt it. **It had transformed it into a skeletal nightmare!**

Sitting atop the horse was a humanoid skeleton. It wore a purple-gray helmet on its head and gripped a bow in its bone-white fist. **It turned its sinister, fleshless face their way.**

By the time Harper realized she should move, the skeleton rider was already firing arrows in their direction.

"RUN!" she cried.

Chapter 5

THE KIDS ARE IN TROUBLE. MAKE NO BONES ABOUT IT!

Jodi's mind was reeling. Ten seconds ago, she had been so happy. She thought there had been a horse! She had immediately started thinking up sweet horse names and trying to remember if anyone had a saddle in their inventory.

Now she and her friends were running for their lives from a skeleton horse and its creepy, arrow-shooting rider. A lot could change in ten seconds!

"I'VE GOT THIS," Morgan said, and he pulled his beloved diamond sword from his inventory. Jodi held her breath as he charged the rider and took a mighty overhead swing. . . .

And his sword bounced harmlessly off the skeleton horseman.

"Oh no," Jodi said. Being unable to harvest resources was one thing. But if they couldn't harm hostile mobs, they were in real trouble.

The skeleton horseman took aim at Morgan. At such a close distance, Morgan was an easy target. The arrow struck him, and he fell back, flashing red as he took damage.

"OUCH!?" he said. "That . . . that isn't fair!"

In the gloom, Jodi saw movement. A figure stepped from a nearby copse of trees. And then another appeared from behind a broken stone pillar. She couldn't make them out until a sudden bolt of lightning provided a moment of light.

There were three of them now. **Of course! she thought. The lightning spawns two additional skeleton horsemen.** And now they were all converging on Morgan.

"THAT'S REALLY NOT FAIR!!!" he complained when he saw the two additional adversaries.

Ash had darted forward. She grabbed Morgan by the shoulder and pulled him back. "Worry about what's fair later!" she said. **"RUN AWAY AND LIVE TO COMPLAIN ANOTHER DAY!"**

"Up here!" Harper said, and she led the others up what was left of the castle's central staircase. Jodi waited long enough to make sure Ash and Morgan were coming; then she turned on her heels and ran after Harper.

It was a long staircase, but not long enough. **Soon the five of them had come to the stone platform at the very top of the tower.** They stood in the open air, rain all around them, and realized they'd arrived at a dead end.

The horsemen wouldn't be far behind.

"What do we do?" Po cried out helplessly. **"WE CAN'T HURT IT!"**

Morgan placed a cobblestone brick on the ground. "Look! We can't break bricks, but we can still place them," he said. **"WE NEED TO PUT UP A BARRIER.** We can build a whole room around ourselves."

"No, stop!" said Harper. "Think about it. **IF YOU BUILD A ROOM AROUND US AND WE CAN'T REMOVE IT LATER, THEN WE'LL BE STUCK.** Anything we build now is permanent!"

"What do we do?" Po cried again, more desperate this time.

"Jodi!" said Ash. "Any ideas? **TELL ME YOU'VE COME UP WITH SOMETHING.**"

Jodi's eyes went wide. "Me? Why me?"

Ash stepped up to Jodi. Everyone else was panicking, but Ash looked eerily calm. "It's what you do best, Jodi. **YOU THINK OUTSIDE THE BOX.**"

Ash's belief in her made Jodi feel a little calmer. She focused on the problem. *Outside the box,* she thought. *Outside the box . . .*

"That's it!" Jodi said. "We don't want to box ourselves in. **WE WANT TO BOX THE BAD GUYS IN.** Build a box!"

As she spoke, their skeletal enemies emerged

from the staircase, leaping right into the middle of the platform. The riders' focus was still on Morgan.

"I'LL KEEP THEM BUSY!" Morgan said, running back and forth. His attackers tried to follow with their bows, but Morgan was too quick.

While the skeletons were distracted, **Jodi and the others leapt into action.** They stacked blocks as quickly as they could, as close to the horses as they dared. By the time the skeletal riders noticed what was happening, the blocks were too high to jump over.

Jodi made a little staircase so that she could reach over the skeletons' head. She placed a final series of blocks on top—a lid for their box.

She hopped back a few steps to admire their handiwork. It looked like a squat chimney made of a variety of mismatched bricks.

"IT ISN'T PRETTY," Jodi said. "But it got the job done."

"It sure did!" said Ash, and she gave Jodi a fist bump. "Good thinking, Jodi."

"I can't believe I almost trapped us in an

inescapable room," Morgan said. "It's like I have to learn a whole new set of rules."

"It's temporary," Ash said. **"WE JUST HAVE TO FIND THE EVOKER KING** and get him to put everything back the way it was."

"Uh, guys?" said Po. "I think I found him."

Jodi followed Po's gaze over the side of the tower. There, in the distance, was a familiar sight: the obsidian words that the Librarian had once built as a warning: **Beware the Evoker King!**

Now, beside those words, something new had been built. It was a great and menacing tower. Jodi thought it looked like a super-villain's headquarters.

"I think you're right, Po," said Jodi. "That's just the sort of place he'd make for himself."

Morgan chuckled darkly. "Dante would love it."

"Whatever happened to him, anyway?" asked Jodi. "I always liked him."

Morgan looked bashful, like he didn't want to answer. He snuck a glance at Ash, and he frowned.

"He moved away," Morgan said sadly. **"AND I NEVER SPOKE TO HIM AGAIN."**

Chapter 6

THE BEST PLANS INVOLVE GHOSTS! WHICH IS IRONIC, BECAUSE GHOSTS AREN'T BIG PLANNERS.

The next day, Harper got to school early. At her request, so did Jodi, Morgan, and Po.

Harper was a problem solver. After all, she loved math and science, and most of the time, *problem solving* was what math and science were all about. There was almost always an answer, a solution. You just had to use the right skills to find it.

That was why she was struggling so much with the news that Ash was moving. If there was a solution to this problem, she couldn't see it. And she wasn't the only one struggling.

Morgan felt the same way. **Their team**

had overcome every challenge it had faced, and Ash's problem should be one more challenge they could overcome.

Po was struggling because he normally laughed in the face of danger. But he couldn't find the humor in this situation.

Jodi seemed to be in denial. She seemed certain that Ash would be in their lives forever.

So, early in the morning, the four of them gathered beneath a great oak tree in the schoolyard. They wanted to discuss their problem. They wanted to *solve* their problem.

"What has everyone come up with?" Harper asked.

"Okay, get this," Po said. "We already put on a great play. What if we did it again? What if we put on a play that was *so convincing* . . . we got everyone to believe that Ash's house is haunted?!"

Harper scrunched her eyebrows. "I don't understand how that would help. **Wouldn't**

that make her parents want to move even more?"

Po gasped. "And leave the poor ghosts behind? Ghosts are the best! Who wouldn't want to live in a haunted house?"

Harper raised her hand, and so did everyone but Po.

"**Well, I like ghosts . . . ,**" he grumbled, crossing his arms.

"I'm thinking about something a little more down-to-earth," said Morgan. "They can't move if they're not able to sell their house. Right?"

Harper thought about it. "I suppose you're right."

"**Okay, so, what if we convince everyone that their house has termites?** No one would buy it then!"

Harper tapped her chin. "I think the only way that would work is if we actually put termites in Ash's house. **And I can't imagine anyone would be very happy about that. . . .**"

"Maybe we can involve the Wildling Scouts somehow?" Jodi asked. "Ash has more merit badges than any of the other scouts, and I know they all look up to her. **What if Ash's troop named her Queen for Life?**"

"I was thinking we could rope in Baron Sweetcheeks," said Harper. "He loves Ash's big playground set. What if we tell them that moving away will cause our class hamster to sink into a deep depression?"

"It won't work," said a voice. They all turned around and saw Ash peek out from behind the tree.

"Ash!" said Po. "How long have you been standing there? I could have used your vote a few minutes ago. . . ."

"I heard most of it," Ash said. "And everything you said made me happy . . . **and sad. . . .**" She looked at each of them in turn. "My mom's job isn't giving her a choice. There's nothing any of us can do to change that. Believe me, I know." She took a deep breath. "But it means the world that you wish that you could fix this. **I've never had friends like you before.**"

"And we've never known anybody like you, Ash," said Morgan.

"Yeah," said Jodi. "We don't want to lose you."

Ash smiled a little. "Well, maybe you don't have to. I mean, not entirely. . . ."

Harper perked up. "You have a solution?" she asked happily.

"I have a different way of thinking about the problem," Ash said. "Listen, we have VR headsets that teleport our minds into a totally realistic version of our favorite video game! It's like magic. We don't *need* to be in the same school or the same town to spend time together."

"The goggles aren't magic," said Harper. "But you've got a good point. A great point."

"You think Doc will let you take a headset with you?" Po asked. "And if you did, you'd be able to connect remotely?"

"I think yes on both counts," said Harper. "Doc will understand, and the technology will work fine."

"That's wonderful!" said Jodi. She crashed against Ash, wrapping her arms around the taller girl and swinging her around in a circle. "We won't be able to hug, but we can still see you and talk to you every day!"

Harper noticed that Morgan wasn't smiling like the rest of them. **"What's wrong,** Morgan?

It's a good plan!"

"It *is* a good plan," Morgan said. "Unless the Evoker King wrecks the game. He's already changed it for the worse."

Ash put her hand on top of Jodi's head. **"Then we just have to stop him.** Don't we?"

Now Morgan smiled. "Yeah. I guess we do."

"Finally," Harper said, feeling the call to action. **"A problem we can solve."**

"Yeah, about that," Ash said. She bit her lip. "I had another idea. But I'm not sure you're going to like this one, Harper."

"Oh?" said Harper. "Why's that?"

"Because we need help to win," said Ash. "And I think that help needs to come from—"

Harper frowned. *"Don't* say Theo."

"Theo," said Ash.

Chapter 7

THE ENEMY OF MY ENEMY IS THIS GUY I KNOW. LET'S GIVE HIM A CHANCE!

Harper still wasn't sure what to make of **Theo Grayson.**

They had started out as friends. Fate (and a class science project) had thrown them together, and they'd found it easy to get along . . . at first. But then Theo messed up their experiment. **And he started acting weird, sneaking around and asking about their Minecraft game.** Morgan had even suspected Theo of being the Evoker King, back before they had discovered that the Evoker King was an artificial intelligence.

Theo obviously wasn't the Evoker King. But Harper and her friends had still never quite come to trust Theo enough to share the secret of the Minecraft goggles. And he had hinted plenty of times that he loved the game, too.

They had worked together again on the school play, and during that time, they had gotten along fine. But Harper had hardly seen him since the play ended. If they were going to ask for his help, she really did owe him an apology for shutting him out.

She found him in the library just after school. She knew he liked to go there to read. She noticed, now, that **the books stacked on the table in front of him were guides to computer programming.**

She hadn't known just how much Theo was into computers and modding until Po revealed that he'd offered his tech skills during the school play.

"**Hey, Theo,**" she said. "What's new?"

Theo looked up, startled. He'd obviously been absorbed in his reading. And it was clear from his expression that **Harper was the last person he expected to see.**

But his startled look was quickly replaced with a goofy smile. "Hey, Harper. It's been a while. You want to sit down?"

Harper smiled back as she took a seat. "I can't stay long. But I'm curious." She looked at the stack of books. "**Po told me you're into programming. Is that right?**"

Theo nodded enthusiastically. He was obviously delighted that she had finally asked him about it. "Yeah! I mean, I know some stuff, but I still have a lot to learn. Computers are complicated."

"**I guess that explains the tower of**

books," said Harper.

"Yeah." Theo blushed. "Although, actually, you caught me goofing off. I was taking a break from reading to review some of my sketches."

"Sketches?" echoed Harper.

"Take a look," he said, and he turned the open book toward her.

Harper saw now that the book in Theo's hand wasn't a library book at all, but **a graph-paper notebook.** Its pages were filled with blocky

drawings. There were blueprints for buildings, and complicated Redstone mechanisms, **and tons of interesting figures in the shape of Minecraft avatars.**

"Wow," Harper said. "You drew all this?"

"Yeah," Theo said. "I like to plan out my Minecraft builds on paper before I make them."

"And the avatars?" Harper asked.

"Oh, I'm getting into modding," Theo said. "You know, using programming to modify the look of the game? Making new skins is the easiest way to start."

Harper flipped the pages. Theo had designed a *lot* of skins. There were reptilian ninjas, robotic monkeys, two-legged dragons, and—

And there, in the back, were a few avatars that Harper recognized.

Theo snatched the book away from her, slamming it shut. "They're just sketches right now," Theo said. "Anyway, do you hear a car honking? I think my mom is here."

Harper blinked, trying to process what she had seen. "I don't hear any—"

"Gotta run," he said. "Bye!"

Theo grabbed his backpack and bolted away, leaving the stack of books behind. Harper thought about going after him. But she was too shocked by what she'd seen in Theo's notebook to even move.

Four of Theo's avatars—she'd seen them before. A knight on a dragon mount. A dark magician. A pirate and an ax-wielding zombie.

Those four mobs had nearly defeated Harper and her friends in the deepest level of the dungeon. Harper knew for a fact they weren't part of any normal game of Minecraft.

How could Theo possibly know about them?

And how could Harper possibly trust him now?

Harper's friends were waiting for her in the computer lab. But they weren't alone. Doc was there, humming happily and bouncing on her toes. And she had put the kids to work.

"These things are heavier than they look," said Morgan. He was straining under the weight of a glass terrarium.

"Yeah, we know," Ash said

with a smirk. "The rest of us carried *two* of them."

Doc helped Morgan ease the terrarium into its place atop a shelf on the back wall. Harper saw now that the terrarium contained a single colorful flower. So did the seven other terrariums lined up on the shelf.

"It looks like a science experiment!" said Harper.

"That's exactly what it is," said Doc. **"Sorry to take over the computer lab.** But these blinds do a good job of keeping out the sunlight. And the air-conditioning keeps this room at a constant seventy-two degrees so that the computers don't overheat."

"I don't understand," said Jodi. "Don't you *want* the flowers to get sunlight?"

"Ah!" said Doc. **"Let's shed some light on that, shall we?"** With that, she flipped a switch, and the terrariums all lit up.

"I should have known," said Po. "Those terrariums are super high-tech!"

"No wonder they're so

heavy," Morgan said, rubbing his triceps.

"These were specially made by yours truly," said Doc. "They provide their own artificial sunlight—along with a precise amount of water, once a day. That way, I can control the exact growing conditions for each flower."

"And *we* can enjoy looking at them!" said Jodi.

"But it seems like a lot of work," said Po. "Why not just put them in the sunlight? Why not just water them yourself?"

Harper knew the answer to that. **"In a science experiment, you have to control all the variables,"** she said. "You don't want to leave anything to random chance."

"That's right," said Doc. "A science experiment is not like life. There are far too many variables in real life. Too much is changing all the time." She chuckled. "Ms. Minerva doesn't like it when things don't go exactly according to plan. **Some people can roll with a bit of chaos, and others can't.** But no matter how you feel about it, there will always be things happening that are out of your control."

"Especially if you're a kid," Ash said, sounding a little sad.

Doc looked thoughtful. "That's true. **At your age, there's very little that you control.** And that can be scary, can't it?"

Harper hadn't really thought of it that way. But Doc was right. It *was* scary to be unable to make your own decisions.

"But there are always things you *can* control," said Doc. **"You can't control how you feel, but you can choose how you act.** You can choose to be kind, compassionate. You can choose to be a good friend. You can choose to look out for one another." She beamed a smile at them. "I can tell that you do that already. You're a good group of kids."

Harper felt her cheeks get warm at the compliment. She still idolized Doc. Even after the trouble the teacher had accidentally unleashed.

In a way, Doc had created the Evoker King, after all. Whether she'd meant to or not.

Talk about not being in control.

"Hey, Harper," Morgan said, and he pulled her aside. "Did you get a chance to talk to Theo?"

Harper frowned. "Not really," she said. "I'll try again later."

She wasn't sure what to make of Theo's sketches. All she knew was that Theo himself was a big question mark. **In scientific terms, he was a variable.** And she couldn't help but wonder what sort of chaos he might unleash if given the chance.

This group of friends was everything to her. **And she wouldn't risk letting an unknown hurt them.**

Not as long as she had any control over the matter.

Chapter 8

THE END CITY: COME FOR THE SIGHTS. STAY BECAUSE YOU'RE TRAPPED. FOREVER!

Ash tried to hide it, but she was worried. Very worried.

She'd always been pretty good at keeping track of the group's inventory. Even with everything split up among them, she usually had a rough idea of how many arrows, apples, and torches they had left.

Right now, they didn't have much. The dungeon delve had pushed them to their limits. **They hadn't worried about it too much,** because they had assumed they'd be able to resupply when they were back on the surface.

So much for that.

She stood now in the shadow of their old castle and watched Morgan try to gnaw on a piece of cooked fish. "It's not working," he said, putting the fillet back into his inventory. "I can't eat. And that means I can't heal the damage I took from the skeleton's arrow."

That isn't good, Ash thought. *It isn't good at all.* But out loud, she said, "That's okay. WE'LL JUST HAVE TO BE REALLY CAREFUL."

She closed her eyes and pulled up her own status bar. Her health was full, but her hunger meter was not. When that meter ran out, she'd start taking damage. **It was the same for all of them.**

They still didn't know what would happen if one of them ran out of health here. Ash really didn't want to find out.

"And you're sure we can't go to Theo?" she asked Harper. "I STILL THINK A PROGRAMMER COULD HELP."

"Maybe a programmer *could* help," said Harper. "But we can't risk asking him. Not until we know what he's hiding."

By then, Ash thought, *it might be too late.* But

out loud, she said, "All right, Harper. It's your call, and I trust you."

Despite low health and mostly unusable items in their inventories, they set out for the block tower in the distance. It was still raining. **With each step, Ash felt gloomier.** It would have been smarter to tunnel through the great hill so they could reach the tower without being easily seen. But that wasn't an option. They had precious few options left to them. What could they do except walk up to the tower and step through its front door?

Ash recognized the tower as an End City a structure typically found in another dimension entirely. Putting the tower square in the middle of the Overworld was just the latest example of the Evoker King's flaunting his powers. She would have call it arrogance . . . except his powers *were* very impressive.

They came upon a waterfall, and Ash gasped

at the sight. The blocks of water had stopped mid-fall. **It was like a 3D sculpture of a waterfall**—utterly still and silent. There was something especially eerie about seeing the water blocks stuck in place while rain still fell from the sky.

The silence was interrupted by the sound of honking. Ash turned to see a villager walking across the grassy field. **His movements were erratic.**

"He's a little far from home," said Po. "The nearest village is a good long walk from here."

"He seems a little . . . *off*," said Harper.

Ash thought Harper was right. **The villager was wandering aimlessly** rather than going anywhere in particular. Even his honking sounded confused and desperate.

"Poor guy," said Jodi. "Maybe he's a farmer who just discovered he can't harvest his crop. Maybe he can't even get his front door open. He must be so confused!"

They all watched as the villager staggered out of view. Then they resumed their journey. The End City grew larger as they drew nearer.

There was another sound, which Ash recognized as clucking. Sure enough, a chicken came into view as it walked atop a nearby hill. It was followed by a cute, blocky chick.

Jodi took a big step back.

"Are you all right, Jodi?" asked Ash. "I don't think I've ever seen you step *away* from an animal before."

"Other than spiders!" said Po.

Jodi frowned. "I'm just afraid a lightning bolt is going to turn that chicken into a razor-beaked attack skeleton," Jodi said. "You know . . . the usual."

The chicken didn't transform, however. It led its chick over the hill and out of sight.

"That little chick will never grow up," said Morgan. "And the mama chicken will never lay another egg."

"You couldn't eat any food," Harper said. **"NEITHER CAN THE ANIMALS."**

Ash knew what they were suggesting. Whatever the Evoker King was up to—whatever his reasons were for doing all this—his actions were having unintended consequences. The entire game world was malfunctioning.

They had to put everything back. **They had to make it right, before it was too late.**

Soon, the End City tower loomed before them. Ash was pretty sure that it was twice as tall as an End City was supposed to be.

Po craned his wizard neck upward to peer through the falling rain. "How much do you want to bet the EK is *alllll* the way up at the top?"

"We could build a big staircase," suggested Harper.

Ash shook her head. **"WE DON'T HAVE NEARLY ENOUGH BLOCKS LEFT.** We used too many getting out of that dungeon chasm and walling up those skeleton riders."

"And I don't think End Cities have any windows," Morgan added. "Since we can't cut or blast our way in, there's no other choice."

"JUST THE BIG, OPEN DOORWAY?" said Po.

"If anybody is suspicious," Jodi said, "we'll just say we're selling Wildling Scout cookies."

"If only I could use my Wildling Scout skin as we enter this obvious trap!" Po complained.

Trap or not, thought Ash, they had to risk it. **The more time went on, the stronger the Evoker King seemed to get. . . .**

And now that they couldn't fix their worn-down weapons or craft new supplies or heal with food or potions, they would only get weaker.

"We have to be more careful than ever," Ash said. **"WE'LL STICK TOGETHER** and take it one room at a time."

The first room was a cavernous entrance hall, all purple and greenish-yellow. The ceiling was high, high, high above them. Between the extreme scale and the weird colors, Ash felt almost queasy.

"The whole thing is made out of purpur blocks," Morgan said. "It's a real End City, all right. **I WONDER IF HE BUILT IT BLOCK BY BLOCK** or if he just pulled the whole thing over from the End dimension."

Ash took a closer look at the walls as they stepped farther into the room. "The thing to remember about purpur blocks," she said, "is that they can hide a hostile mob called—"

"SHULKER!" Morgan called. **"LOOK OUT!"**

Ash saw it then. One of the purpur blocks popped open. It was hollow, and inside it was a small, pale creature, cube-shaped, with big eyes.

"It's sort of cute," said Jodi.

"IT'S DANGEROUS!" said Ash. She started dropping blocks. "We need to build a barrier!"

Within seconds, **Ash had constructed a short wall between them and the shulker.** But she had forgotten something important.

A shulker's energy blasts could find them wherever they hid.

A glowing trail of energy flew right over the wall, striking Jodi in the back. She flashed red, taking damage . . . and then, right before Ash's eyes, Jodi started to float into the air.

"Um?" said Jodi. **"GOOD THING, OR BAD THING?"**

"Bad thing!" Morgan cried, and he grabbed for Jodi's foot to keep her from floating away.

But the shulker had fired five energy blasts.
They all found their targets.

Ash found herself floating into the air beside her friends.

"This doesn't seem so bad," said Po.

"You know the old saying," Morgan said, flailing around. "What comes up must come down."

Ash knew Morgan was right. **The levitation effect would only last about ten seconds.** But in that time, they would rise higher and higher. And after that . . .

Well. It would be a long way to fall.

Chapter 9

A MOMENT THAT WAS LONG OVERDUE: THE LIBRARIAN COMES TO THE RESCUE!

Po dragged his blocky hands against the walls. He couldn't find anything to grab hold of. **He kept floating up, up. . . .**

And the ground kept getting farther away.

"This is going to be some major fall damage," he said.

"Can't we do anything to soften the landing?" Ash said.

"I still have a few potions of slow falling," Harper said. "But we can't drink potions anymore."

"WAIT, LOOK DOWN THERE!" cried Jodi. "What is that?"

Po squinted. Down below, he could see a strange

pixelation effect. The air itself seemed to shimmer.

Then there was a loud *pop,* and a familiar figure stood on the ground.

It was the Librarian!

"I'm here?" she said. She looked at her blocky hands. "I'm here! He did it!"

Who did what? Po wondered. But he was certainly glad to see her. The Librarian looked like an average villager, **but she was smart and very good at gathering resources.** She'd been aiding them since the very beginning of their adventures.

And they could sure use some aid now.

"HELP!" Po cried. **"WE'RE UP HERE!"**

The Librarian looked up. Her eyes went wide when she saw them floating there. "Stay put!" she said. "I need to take care of this shulker first."

"You can't damage it," Ash warned her.

"I don't need to," said the Librarian. She produced a water bucket from her inventory. **"YOU KNOW WHAT HAPPENS WHEN YOU GET A SHULKER WET, DON'T YOU?"**

"Oh," Morgan said. "Of course. That's brilliant!"

"What?" Po said. "What happens when you get a shulker wet?"

He watched as the Librarian doused the mob with her bucket of water. **As soon as the water touched it, the shulker teleported away.**

"*That* happens," said the Librarian.

She didn't pause to celebrate her victory, though. She immediately set to work building a column, leaping into the air and placing bricks beneath her feet, one after the other. She had almost reached them when Po felt a lurching sensation in his stomach.

They weren't levitating anymore. **They were falling!**

The Librarian stopped building her column. She now focused on building *out* instead of *up,* creating a flat block structure high above the ground.

Po fell onto the platform, and his friends all landed nearby. It didn't hurt, because they hadn't fallen very far.

He peered over the edge of the platform. The ground was far below them. *That* would have hurt.

"Thanks for the help," he said.

"I'm just glad I got here in time," she said.

"The Evoker King found a way to lock me out. But I've got a hacker on my side—**AND HE WAS ABLE TO FIND A WEAKNESS IN THE KING'S FIREWALL.**"

"So you're *not* another artificial consciousness," Harper said. "You're a person. You've got the missing sixth headset!"

"That's right," said the Librarian. **"I KNEW SOMETHING WAS WONKY ABOUT DOC'S INVENTION,** and I wanted to make sure you were all safe. You've probably guessed my identity by now."

"ARE YOU THE LUNCH LADY?" Po guessed. "The principal? Oh my gosh. Are you Amelia Earhart? So that's what happened to you!"

"You're Ms. Minerva," said Morgan. "Aren't you?"

The Librarian smiled. "You're right."

Po's mouth hung open. Their teacher had been helping them all along? She'd been the one filling chests with valuable resources and top-tier enchanted weapons?

"Ms. Minerva," he said. **"YOU . . . ARE REALLY GOOD AT MINECRAFT."**

"Why, thank you," she said. "But don't sound so surprised. I've been playing video games since 1995 or so." Her smile dropped away. "But I've never encountered anything like the Evoker King. I'm deeply curious about what he's up to, and why. **So far, you five have handled everything he's thrown at you."** She sighed. "But he's never had so much power. Are you sure you want to confront him? We could put aside our headsets and walk away."

The group exchanged silent glances. They

hadn't said it out loud, but they all knew that was an option. They could walk away and let the Evoker King have this virtual world.

But this place felt like their own secret playhouse. A sandbox of infinite possibility, where they'd had the most memorable adventures of their lives.

AND NOW IT WAS THEIR BEST CHANCE OF GETTING TO SEE ASH, EVEN IF SHE MOVED HALFWAY AROUND THE WORLD.

"We can't give up now," Po said, and he knew from their nods that his friends agreed. "We love this place, and we can't let the Evoker King

ruin it or scare us away."

Ms. Minerva's librarian avatar smiled once more. "I hoped you'd say that. **I NEVER COULD TURN AWAY FROM A MYSTERY.** And this place is quite a mystery. You deserve a chance to explore it without the Evoker King running the show."

"And now that you're here, you can help us!" said Ash.

"I WOULDN'T BE MUCH HELP," said the teacher. **"WHILE THE EVOKER KING HAS THE FOUNDATION STONE, I CAN'T DO ANY MORE THAN YOU CAN.** You don't need me . . . you need my secret weapon."

"THE HACKER," Harper said. She sounded suspicious.

"Exactly," said Ms. Minerva. "And there are only six headsets. So I'm going to give him mine now. But I'll be watching over you from the computer lab, just like always."

"Thank you," said Ash. "Thank you for helping us. But also . . . thank you for trusting us to fix this."

She nodded. **"YOU'RE A VERY CAPABLE GROUP OF STUDENTS. PARTICULARLY WHEN YOU WORK TOGETHER AS A TEAM. I ONLY HOPE THERE'S ROOM ON YOUR TEAM FOR ONE MORE. . . ."**

With that, the Librarian disappeared in a burst of pixels. They all waited for the hacker to appear. Po could hardly contain his nervous energy.

Finally, the air rippled once more with pixels, and Po and his friends saw their new teammate. **They all gasped.** The avatar was instantly recognizable.

The hacker was . . .

Chapter 10

WELCOME TO THE TEAM!
I HOPE YOU SURVIVE
THE EXPERIENCE.

Theo!!!

Theo was here, with them. **Theo was the hacker!**

Harper couldn't believe her eyes. But then again, why *should* she believe them? Just because the avatar looked like Theo, that didn't mean Theo was the player behind the avatar.

"DON'T WORRY, GUYS," he said. "I'm here to solve all your problems!"

Okay, thought Harper. *That is* definitely *the real Theo.*

"Hey, man!" said Po. **"WELCOME TO THE PARTY."**

"Hold up," said Harper. "We need to talk about some things first. You mean to tell me you've been working with Ms. Minerva this whole time?"

"I wish I had been," said Theo. "That would have helped you avoid some trouble. **BUT I'VE BEEN ON MY OWN UNTIL RECENTLY."**

"Start at the beginning," said Ash. "Tell us everything."

Theo nodded. "For me, **IT STARTED WHEN THE EVOKER KING INFILTRATED THE SCHOOL'S SYSTEMS.** I noticed right away that something was up with the computers, and I did some digging in the code. **FROM WHAT I SAW, IT WAS PRETTY OBVIOUS THAT WE'D BEEN HACKED."**

"What did you do?" asked Morgan.

"I went straight to Ms. Minerva," he answered. "And

that's when things got really interesting."

Theo paused for dramatic effect.

Harper huffed. "Just tell us what happened, Theo!" she said.

"All right, all right! Ms. Minerva knew more than she was willing to tell me. But she was impressed with my hacking skills, and she asked me to take a look at a VR headset . . . and the server that was running your Minecraft game. **I COULD SEE WHERE DOC'S TINKERING HAD CAUSED SOME STRANGE THINGS TO HAPPEN.** The source of all the strangeness was a key bit of code in Doc's modifications. A programmer would call it a bug. You call it . . . the Foundation Stone."

"SO THE FOUNDATION STONE IS THE SOURCE OF ALL THE WEIRDNESS?" Morgan asked. "Even before the Evoker King started messing with us, we noticed that this world wasn't exactly like a standard game of Minecraft."

"For instance," said Jodi, "I can do handstands." She did one, to illustrate her point. Po clapped his square hands and said, **"YOU CAN'T DO THAT IN VANILLA MINECRAFT."**

Theo began to pace on the platform. "That's right. The bug is like this . . . little seed of possibility. **IT MAKES THIS PLACE A LITTLE MORE WEIRD AND A LITTLE MORE WONDERFUL."**

"I still think it might be magic," Po said. "I'm like ninety-five percent sure." Harper knocked him lightly on the head while Theo continued.

"IN OTHER WORDS, THE BUG-THE FOUNDATION STONE-IS ACTUALLY HAVING A POSITIVE EFFECT. That seed was flowering and evolving the game to have new possibilities. You're having *more* fun because of it, not less. But you had to be *inside* to know that. From the outside looking in—just looking at how the code was working—it just looked like a mistake. **A flaw in the system.** And Doc's goal as an inventor is to correct her mistakes—and to *eliminate* flaws."

"How would she do that?" asked Ash.

"With a tool she's used before: artificial intelligence." Theo smirked. "She introduced the Evoker King into the game's code. She gave it a simple command: find what was wrong and fix it.

GET RID OF THE CHAOS. IMPOSE ORDER!"

"So why hasn't he done that?" asked Morgan. "What went wrong?"

"*You* did," said Theo. "The AI's mission got a lot more complicated when a bunch of kids showed up and started moving things around at random. Building. Exploring. Causing change. **MY THEORY IS THAT YOUR APPEARANCE FORCED THE AI TO EVOLVE. IT BECAME THE EVOKER KING.** But he still had the same mission. He had wanted to find and neutralize the Foundation Stone . . . but at some point, he decided to use it instead. He must have realized that he could weaponize it against the greater threat. **YOU.**"

"**THAT IS . . . A LOT TO PROCESS,**" said Ash.

"So Ms. Minerva brought *you* in, and you built the dungeon?" Harper asked Theo. "And you reskinned the mobs we fought there?"

"Yeah, but you were never supposed to fight them. **I WAS TRYING TO KEEP THE EVOKER KING AWAY FROM THE FOUNDATION STONE.** He's actually not very creative. So my dungeon worked . . . until you guys cracked it wide open, defeated the guardians, and left the way open for the Evoker King."

"**OOPS,**" said Jodi.

"Yeah," said Po. "Our bad!"

Theo shrugged. "Live and learn. If I'd told Ms. Minerva about my dungeon plan, she wouldn't have sent you there. I guess this is what being secretive gets you."

He didn't say it, but Harper knew what he was thinking: **If she hadn't insisted on keeping their game a secret** from Theo, they could have been working together all along.

Harper was glad avatars couldn't blush.

"I'm still trying to wrap my head around the Foundation Stone being a bug," said Po. "I thought it was, like . . . a stone."

"IT'S REALLY A PIECE OF CODE," said Theo. "A string of ones and zeroes."

"That hunk of rock?" said Jodi. "It's made of, like . . . math?"

"Remember," said Theo, getting really excited as he talked, "you're inside a virtual world made by machines. **THE FOUNDATION STONE AND THIS PLATFORM WE'RE STANDING ON AND THAT WALL OVER THERE—THEY LOOK LIKE PHYSICAL OBJECTS. BUT IT'S ALL MADE OUT OF COMPUTER CODE.** And the code that makes up the Foundation Stone is like a key that unlocks the programming of this entire world. It's the ultimate super-hack! It's . . . it's . . . **THE SLASH COMMAND OF THE GODS!"**

"Okay. Okay. We get it," said Morgan. "The

Evoker King's always been able to bend the rules," Morgan said. "But now, with the Stone, he's not limited to just bending the rules. He can break them."

"Right," said Theo. **"FORTUNATELY, I'M ABLE TO BEND A RULE OR TWO MYSELF."** He turned to Harper. "You said you've got slow-fall potions? Try drinking one now."

Harper did as Theo suggested. As soon as she took a sip, she felt instantly lighter. "It's working. We can apply status effects again."

Theo nodded. **"YEAH. I'M RUNNING A MOD** that lets me ignore the Evoker King's tampering. As long as you're within a few blocks of me, you're not locked out anymore."

"Then we can eat," Ash said.

"WE CAN HEAL!" Morgan added, and he devoured a bowl of soup.

"And more important—I don't have to be a wizard anymore!" Po said happily. He winked out of existence, then immediately reappeared in the form of a boxer. "Let's take this fight to the Evoker King!"

Harper heard a high-pitched horn sound from above. She looked up and saw movement against the shadowed ceiling. "Careful what you wish for, Po," she said, quickly passing out potions to the others. "It looks like our enemy's sent a welcome party!"

A vex swooped down from the shadows, flapping its tattered wings and raising its sword.

"It has the advantage up here," said Ash. "Everybody get to the ground before our potions wear off!"

"Don't worry, guys," said Theo. "I've got this."

EVERYBODY LEAPED OFF THE PLATFORM. But while Harper and the others floated slowly downward, Theo jumped straight up. He rose higher than Harper had ever seen anyone jump before!

"I've got a double-jump mod on my avatar," said Theo. "And check *this* out."

In midair, Theo held up a sword. **It was made of wood—the most basic weapon you could get.** Harper knew it would take a lot of hits with that thing to hurt a vex.

But Theo's sword shimmered for a moment. When the shimmering stopped, the wooden sword had become diamond. **It sliced through the air, doing massive damage to the vex.**

"Ha!" Theo laughed as he landed back on the platform. He raised his sword above his head and whooped. "I am the hack master!"

"Ugh," said Morgan as he touched down on the ground beside Harper. "Are we *sure* this guy isn't the Evoker King?"

"Be nice, Morgan," Jodi said, scolding him.

"Very impressive, Theo!" Harper called up at him. **"BUT YOU MIGHT WANT TO WATCH YOUR BACK!"**

Harper's warning was too late. The vex swooped down, slashing Theo in the back.

"Ouch!" he said. "I felt that!"

So he's not invincible, thought Harper. *He's just got a few tricks. Probably all stuff he had to program in advance.*

Theo focused on defeating the vex. **With his diamond sword at the ready, it was no contest.** Afterward, he made his way down from the platform, using a pickaxe to mine straight down through the column that Ms. Minerva had built.

"OKAY, IT WASN'T A FLAWLESS VICTORY," Theo said once he was on the ground with them. "But you can see how I'll be helpful, right?"

Harper and Morgan shared a look.

"Yeah, okay," said Morgan.

"WELCOME TO THE TEAM, THEO," said Harper.

"All right!" said Theo. Even though their avatar voices tended to be kind of plain and flat, they could hear the genuine enthusiasm in Theo's voice. He had been waiting for this. "I am so ready to fight our way through this tower."

"NOT SO FAST," said Ash. "Now that you're here, we may have other options. . . ."

"And we've learned that the best path isn't always the one that goes right through danger,"

added Morgan. "Especially considering that the **EVOKER KING HAS A WEAKNESS.**"

"He does?" Po said.

"He does," Harper confirmed. "Remember? **AS AN ARTIFICIAL INTELLIGENCE, HE'S VERY SMART ... BUT NOT VERY CREATIVE.**"

"Which is why he couldn't get through my dungeon," Theo said. "It took *you* guys to figure out a way past the guardians."

"Huh," Po said. He rubbed his blocky chin. **"SO IT WOULD BE PRETTY EASY TO PLAY A PRANK ON HIM,** I guess."

Harper liked the sound of that. "You have an idea, Po?" she asked.

"I think I do," he said. "But we're going to have to split up. And we're going to need some *bait*."

"What kind of bait?" asked Jodi. "We still don't have any cookies. . . ."

"I had something else . . . **SOMEONE** else in mind," Po said. He gave Theo a long look. "Just how badly do you think the Evoker King would like to get his hands on our little hacker friend?"

THEO GAVE A LOUD GULP.

Chapter 11

EVEN AN ARTIFICIAL INTELLIGENCE CAN MAKE A MISTAKE . . . AND HAVE BAD BREATH!

Morgan liked this plan.

It was risky, sure. But it was probably less risky than fighting their way through the Evoker King's fortress.

And he didn't love the fact that they'd had to split up. It was going to be just three of them against a power-mad artificial consciousness, and he didn't love those odds.

Of course, that was assuming they could even get the King's attention. . . .

"I think this'll do it," said Ash. "Don't you?"

"Oh, yeah," said Theo. **"THERE'S NO WAY HE CAN IGNORE THIS."**

Morgan looked up at their handiwork. Where huge obsidian letters had once spelled out a warning—*Beware the Evoker King*—they now spelled out something else entirely.

Beware the Evoker King's Bad Breath.

"It's a true work of art," said Morgan.

"Then I guess we're ready," said Ash. "Hit it!"

"OH, EVOOOOOKER KING," crooned Theo. "We're down here!"

"We know you can see us!" yelled Morgan.

"Just look at what Theo has done to your beautiful sign!" cried Ash.

They waited to see what would happen. Except for the rain, the world was still and silent. Morgan started to worry. Maybe the Evoker King wasn't at home. Maybe he wasn't going to take the bait.

He needn't have worried. **There was a great flash of light, and a sound like thunder.** For just a moment, Morgan thought it was the storm. But then he saw the jagged hole at the top of the tower and the shadowy figure who stood within it. The Evoker King had blasted a hole right through his own wall.

Morgan felt a rush of nervousness as he laid eyes on the Evoker King at last. **He ... or it ... looked nothing like Morgan had expected.** The Evoker King was more menacing than before.

The AI's outer layer was now transparent, and he crackled with energy both inside and out. Morgan could see *inside* the figure.

Rather than organs or muscles or blood or Minecraft blocks, **the Evoker King's see-through skin contained swirling pixels of light.** He looked like a living galaxy—a digital constellation given humanoid shape. His eyes glowed with malice.

"HOW DARE YOU!" boomed the voice of the Evoker King, and spirals of wild energy sparkled and swirled around his fists. The lights in his chest pulsated with power, and his facial features flickered as he spoke. Now, as he scowled down at them, his face seemed more monstrous than before.

MORGAN HAD TO FIGHT A SUDDEN DESIRE TO RUN AND HIDE.

"You just can't help yourselves, can you?" said their foe. He was floating above their heads, just out of reach. "You're worse than a wild band of creepers. You bring chaos everywhere you go! You break and you take whatever you want. You disrupt the natural order!"

"You're one to talk!" said Morgan. **"TAKE A LOOK AT WHAT YOU'VE DONE SINCE YOU GOT THE FOUNDATION STONE."**

"Morgan's right," said Ash. "You've broken the world!"

"I've *fixed* the world!" said the King. "I made it so that nothing would ever change again. **NO MORE CHAOS!** Only order!" "The Evoker King turned his flat digital eyes on Theo. "And then *you* came along. You did this, didn't you? You found a way to break *my* rules!"

"**I SURE DID!**" said Theo. "Me, Theo! **I HAVE COOL HACKING SKILLS!** You want to see them in action?"

"I've seen enough," said the Evoker King. That high-pitched horn sounded again, and three vexes appeared.

That, at least, is a typical evoker move, Morgan thought.

But then the Evoker King summoned zombies. And **skeletons.** And armed and angry **illagers.**

In the time it took Morgan to blink, he and his friends were hopelessly surrounded.

"You have one final choice to make," said the King. "Disconnect now . . . or fall to my hordes."

"**I'M TERRIBLE AT MAKING CHOICES,**" said Theo.

"We're not leaving!" said Ash. "Because we're right, and you're wrong. Minecraft is supposed to be for *everyone.*"

"**WE'RE FIGHTING FOR A WORLD OF**

FREEDOM AND CREATIVITY!" cried Morgan. "The way it's meant to be!"

"So be it." With pulse of energy, the Evoker King set his minions to attack.

The three friends drew their swords. They dodged and darted, ducked and danced to stay out of reach of their attackers.

But there were too many of them. And Morgan's sword was useless against them. He couldn't hurt them.

The mobs could hurt *him*, however. He flashed red with each punch and slash and bite. **He saw Ash and Theo taking damage, too.**

Theo's presence had allowed them to get their health up to full strength before the fight, but it was draining quickly. How much could they take before they fell?

"We have to get out of here," Morgan said.

"No!" said Ash. **"THE OTHERS . . . THEY NEED MORE TIME."**

"Then I'd better do something foolish," said Theo. "Hey, Evoker King! Too scared to face me on your own?"

"Scared?" said the King. **"YOU THINK I'M SCARED? OF YOU?"**

With a wave of the Evoker King's hand, the

teeming hordes stopped in their tracks. Morgan poked a zombie with his sword and got no response.

"Actually," said Theo, "now that you mention it . . . I think maybe you're scared. You're so desperate to push us around . . . to get rid of us . . ."

"Enough," said the Evoker King. **THE GROUND BENEATH THEM RUMBLED.** Morgan and Ash fell back, but Theo was caught in a rising flood of dirt and stone blocks.

The Evoker King had shaped the very ground into an enormous stony hand that quickly became a fist. **It held Theo in its grip, lifting him off his feet.** "I'll show you something to fear," said their enemy.

"Do your . . . worst," said Theo.

"No, stop!" said Morgan. **"DON'T HURT HIM!"**

"I'll do whatever I want," said the King. The stone fist tightened. Theo cried out.

Suddenly, the Evoker King froze. **His eyes narrowed in suspicion.** "Why aren't you saving yourself?" he asked. "Why aren't you using your great powers?"

"Because . . . ," said Theo through clenched teeth. "Because . . . I'm not . . . Theo."

The Evoker King's eyes grew large with surprise. **"WHAT?!"**

Theo blinked out of existence. Because it wasn't Theo at all, but a Theo skin.

And now Po was there, grinning at the Evoker King.

"GOTCHA," he said.

Chapter 12

MEANWHILE: STEALTH SQUAD IS GO!

Jodi gripped her trident tightly and hoped that her brother was safe.

She knew he was risking his neck so she and Harper and Theo—the *real* Theo—had a chance at ending this fight once and for all.

"THIS PLAN IS BANANAS," said Theo.

"Yeah," agreed Jodi. "That's why it's brilliant. The Evoker King will never see it coming!"

"And what's the signal?" Theo asked. **"WHAT EXACTLY ARE WE WAITING FOR?"**

"We should know it when we see it," said Harper.

The three of them were crouching behind a low

wall on the far side of the tower. While they stayed
out of view, Morgan and Ash and Po were uphill,
standing out in the open and making a lot of noise.

**They had to draw out the Evoker
King.** But would it work?

There was an explosion at the top of the tower. Jodi almost yelped in surprise, but she stopped herself. Stealth mode, she reminded herself.

But she almost yelped again when she saw the Evoker King. He was standing in the gaping hole he'd just made in the side of his own tower. She watched as he stepped through the hole and slowly floated down toward Morgan and the others. Even at this distance, she could tell he was angry.

"That's our cue," Harper said. **"GO! GO! GO!"**

"Finally," Jodi said. "Do you know how long it's been since I got to fly?"

Jodi hurled her trident in the air, and it pulled her along for the ride, lifting her right off the ground and sending her hurtling across the sky.

"WAHOO!" cried Harper beside her. "This is amazing!"

"And sort of terrifying!" yelled Theo.

Jodi had flown all the time back when she played Minecraft in Creative mode. It wasn't quite so simple here.

They had gotten lucky with the weather. According to Morgan, this trick was only possible underwater . . . or in the rain. **With Theo's help, Harper had enchanted three tridents with a magical riptide effect.** The effect basically allowed them to swim through the wet air. It would get them to the top of the tower *quickly*. And right now, every minute counted.

So it was nice that the Evoker King had made an opening for them.

"IN HERE!" said Jodi, and she flew through the hole the Evoker King had left. Harper and

Theo touched down close behind her.

Jodi had expected more of the purpur blocks they'd seen downstairs. Or perhaps a lush sanctuary—tapestries and artworks and a four-poster bed fit for a king.

But there was none of that. Instead, the room was a cold and sterile box. Four plain white walls met a plain white ceiling and a plain white floor. **The only thing in the room was a pale-colored**

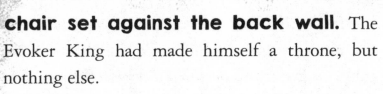

chair set against the back wall. The Evoker King had made himself a throne, but nothing else.

"What material is this?" asked Harper, stomping her foot. "It looks almost like glass, but not quite."

"It's nothing that exists naturally in the game," Theo said. **"HE'S LEACHED THE COLOR AND TEXTURE OUT OF EVERYTHING."**

"It looks like something an emotionless computer program would make," Jodi said. "No color, no joy . . . no personal touches of chaos." She shuddered. "I bet he'd like to do this to the whole world."

"WE WON'T LET HIM," Theo said confidently. "We just have to find the Foundation Stone before he comes back."

Harper held up a pickaxe. "Then let's get digging—and hope that he keeps it close!"

Jodi figured Harper had the right idea. If there was a hidden vault around here, it would be on the other side of a wall or floor. **They all took up pickaxes.** As long as they stayed near Theo, they were able to break as many bricks as they wanted.

They made a mess of the place, busting holes in every surface. They didn't find any hidden passages or trapdoors, only more of the strange white blocks. **The walls and floor were thick but otherwise unremarkable.**

"I don't know where else to look," said Harper. "I was sure he'd keep it by his seat of power."

"SEAT . . . OF POWER?" echoed Jodi.

"It's just another way of saying 'throne,'" said Theo.

"Huh," said Jodi. She took a closer look at it. Now that she'd gotten used to all the whiteness, she saw something she hadn't noticed before. "Did you notice how his throne is sort of . . . glowing?"

"THE THRONE!" said Theo, pointing. "The Foundation Stone is that block right in the middle of the throne!"

"What have you done *now*?" said a voice.

They whirled around to see the Evoker King floating just outside the tower. He looked furious.

"YOU HAVE INVADED MY HOME.

DESTROYED IT. YOU BRING DESTRUCTION
WHEREVER YOU GO!"

"I don't know about destruction," said Jodi.
"I'm sort of in a *creation* mood."

She spun around and ran for the throne.

"No!" cried the King. **"STOP!"**

The Evoker King was faster than Jodi.

But Jodi was closer.

She could see him out of the corner of her eye.
He was gaining on her. They were neck and
neck.

He reached out for the throne.

So did she. She stretched out her arms, leaping,
and . . .

**Jodi's blocky hand touched the
Foundation Stone first.**

Chapter 13

LITTLE SISTERS. THEY GROW UP SO FAST! ESPECIALLY WHEN THEIR MINDS EXPAND TO ENCOMPASS AN ENTIRE WORLD!

Jodi's vision went white.

She no longer felt her body. **Or rather, she felt her body everywhere.**

She was a waterfall that had been frozen in time.

She was a stone fist, gripping Po tightly.

She was a llama in a field. She was an ocelot on a rooftop. She was a bale of hay, being eaten by a horse. **It tickled!**

She was a forest, and all the trees that made the forest. She was a desert, and every bit of shifting scratchy sand within it.

She was water, and lava, and stone. She was in every block, every torch,

every glittering gem.

She was Minecraft. And Minecraft was her.

Jodi could see the strings of digits that made up the code behind the world. She could see where the Evoker King had twisted that code—the cut he'd made here, the addition over there. She put things back the way they were supposed to be. **For her, it was as easy as arranging a set of colorful building blocks.**

She was a waterfall, flowing once more into a moving river.

She was a fist, relaxing its grip, becoming an open palm.

And she was an evoker, standing in a broken throne room, trembling with emotion. Jodi recognized that emotion. . . .

It was *fear.*

The Evoker King was so afraid he could barely stand it.

Chapter 14

THE KING HAS FALLEN. LONG LIVE THE QUEEN!

Morgan didn't know what to expect when he, Ash, and Po entered the Evoker King's throne room. **As they built a zigzagging staircase to the top of the tower,** he tried to prepare himself for anything.

But he was still shocked at the sight of his sister floating inches off the ground and glowing with tremendous power.

"Jodi!" he cried. "Are you all right?"

"I'VE NEVER BEEN BETTER," said Jodi. Her voice boomed. "This is like ultimate Creative mode!" With a wave of her hand, Jodi fixed every bit of damage in the throne room. Then she added

some colorful tapestries and a purple llama for good measure.

"Then what are you waiting for?" asked Theo. He pointed to the Evoker King. **"GET RID OF HIM!** Make him disappear!"

The Evoker King glared. Without the power of the stone, he had become something of a basic avatar—like his throne room, he was plain and lacking detail. "Do your worst!" he grumbled.

"I'M NOT GOING TO HURT YOU,"

Jodi said. "I promise. I know you're afraid."

"I'm . . . I'm not afraid!" he protested. "I am beyond such things."

"You are afraid. I can . . . I can feel your fear," said Jodi. "We assumed that you wouldn't have emotion. **We thought you were just a program,** and a villainous program, at that." She frowned and shook her head. "But you were here first. And you were happy here, in a world of simple rules, where everything made sense. Then we came along. YOU DIDN'T KNOW WHAT TO MAKE OF A GROUP OF MESSY, LOUD HUMANS who started moving stuff around and chopping down trees and beating up monsters and filling treasure chests."

"And using dye to color sheep," said Po. "I bet that really confused him."

Morgan's head spun. "JODI, ARE YOU SURE ABOUT THIS?"

"I'm with Morgan," said Harper. "He's an artificial intelligence. Why should he be afraid? Why should he feel anything?"

"HE'S A VERY YOUNG ARTIFICIAL

INTELLIGENCE," Jodi said. "Younger than us. He's still growing. Learning. *Becoming*."

"But what will he become?" Morgan asked.

"I WILL BECOME YOUR GREATEST NIGHTMARE!" said the Evoker King. "I shall be vengeance incarnate!"

"Oh, stop that." Jodi chuckled. "I think what you might become . . . is our friend," she said.

The Evoker King gaped. "How could we be friends?" he said. "My purpose is to bring order to this world. And you are forces of chaos!"

 "YOU SHOULD CHOOSE YOUR OWN PURPOSE," said Jodi. "You've already changed your mind about the Foundation Stone. At first you wanted to destroy it, but then you used it. Maybe you could change your mind about us, too."

Morgan turned to the others. "What's she talking about?" he asked. "I MEAN, CAN A HUMAN AND AN ARTIFICIAL INTELLIGENCE EVEN BE FRIENDS?"

"I think she's got an interesting point," said

Theo. "The Evoker King has shown that he's capable of learning. His programming is changing as he encounters new things. Friendship could be a total game changer for him." Theo snuck Harper a bashful glance. "He might have been rude or selfish in the past. But maybe he just needs a second chance."

"It makes a lot of sense to me," said Ash. **"I KNOW WHAT IT FEELS LIKE TO BE AFRAID OF CHANGE.** To wish you could control everything because you feel like you're not in control of anything. I know exactly what it feels like." She turned her eyes on the Evoker King. "It's *terrifying*. But it's a little less scary when you have friends."

"Wouldn't you rather try to understand us?" said Jodi. "Wouldn't that be more logical than fighting? **THINK OF ALL THE GREAT THINGS WE COULD BUILD TOGETHER!"**

The Evoker King stood very still. Morgan couldn't read his expression. The AI looked from Jodi to Theo, and then at each of them in turn. "To be honest, when I used the Foundation Stone to build this tower, I felt a . . . a thrill. And I felt something similar when I crafted the first avatar for myself."

"That's the thrill that comes with being creative," said Jodi. "It can be messy and chaotic, but in the end, **CREATING NEW THINGS— ART OR INVENTIONS OR STORIES OR FRIENDSHIPS—IS THE BEST WAY WE HAVE TO MAKE THE WORLD A BETTER PLACE.**"

Morgan found that he agreed with her. "Creation helps us make sense of a messy world," he added.

The Evoker King smiled shyly. "This is all very

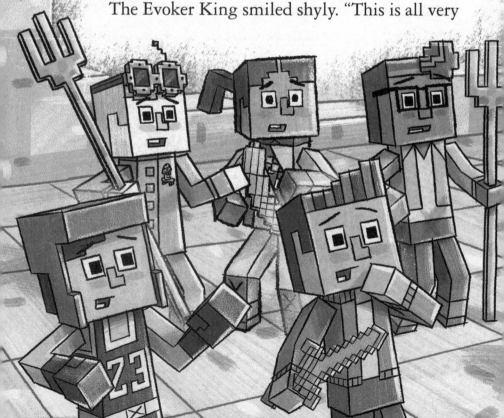

interesting to me. I have much to consider." He turned his gaze toward Jodi. **"I . . . WOULD LIKE VERY MUCH TO HAVE YOU AS FRIENDS, I THINK."**

"And none of that vengeance incarnate stuff, right?" Jodi asked.

The Evoker King tried to hold her gaze with his fiercest look, but then he timidly replied, "No. No vengeance incarnate stuff."

"Then it's settled," said Jodi. **"SO SAYS QUEEN JODI, RULER OF MINECRAFT!"**

And she laughed a deep, dark, sinister laugh. Morgan's blood ran cold as the sound of echoed through the halls.

"You guys!" Jodi said in her normal voice. *"I'm totally joking!"*

"We're putting the Foundation Stone back where we found it," said Morgan.

"Oh yes," said Ash. **"DEEP UNDERGROUND."**

Harper nodded. "Theo, you can be in charge of building a new dungeon to keep it safe."

"AW, I WAS HOPING I'D GET A TURN WITH IT," said Po.

"No!" they all cried at once.

The Evoker King looked at Theo. "Are they always like this?" he asked.

"DON'T ASK ME," said Theo. **"I'M NEW, TOO."**

Chapter 15

TO ALL THINGS, AN ENDING. BUT IN EVERY ENDING, A NEW BEGINNING. (AND CAKE, SOMETIMES!)

It was Ash's last day at Woodsword Middle School.

She had emptied her locker. She'd returned her textbooks and packed up her gym clothes.

All that was left now was to say goodbye.

They all gathered in the computer lab. Harper had made a "science cake," which was what she called all cakes. Jodi had put up streamers. Doc and Ms. Minerva were there, and they told Ash how much they would miss her. Ash thought she saw Morgan cry a little, but he denied it later.

"I want you to have this," said Doc. She handed

Ash a set of VR goggles with a big red bow on top. **"Ms. Minerva tells me all the glitches have been fixed, thanks to you."**

"Yes, no more glitches," Ms. Minerva said, adding a very unsubtle wink.

"What was that?" Doc asked. "Why did you wink just then?"

"Oh, just being a bit chaotic, Doc," said Ms. Minerva. "I know how much you enjoy that."

"Thanks for these," Ash said, holding the goggles to her chest. "Thanks for *everything*. **I've had just ... just the best time here.** My new school won't be the same."

"But it's just a few towns over," said Theo. "We can see you on weekends."

"And virtually every weekday," said Jodi, pointing to the headset.

"We're never more than a call away," Harper added. She held up her old phone, which she'd had to quit using when the Evoker King had taken over the school's tech. Now, with a little help from Doc and Theo, it was working better than ever.

Ash laughed. "Yeah. I guess so."

"You're taking it well, though, Ash," said Doc. "This can't be easy for you."

"It's not," said Ash. **"It's sad, and scary, and totally out of my control."** She smiled, just a little. "But I've got friends to help me through it."

"Aw, gee," said Po. "You're going to make the rest of us cry like Morgan."

"I wasn't crying!" Morgan protested, quickly pulling his hand away from the corner of his eye. "I have allergies!"

"And I have a present for you," Ash said. "All of you. The whole school, actually!"

Ash led them outside and across the schoolyard.

They passed the bat house they'd built together some time ago, and they kept walking. "I couldn't put it *too* close to the bat house," she said. "That might have caused some problems if the bats decided to take up residence." She laughed as she led them farther down the path and around the back of the school's mobile classrooms. She heard them all gasp when they saw her surprise.

"It's your tree house!" said Morgan. "How in the world did you move it here?"

"Well, my mom's an engineer, remember?" said Ash. "I know how much you all love it. So I thought it would be a nice gift."

"It's the best gift," Jodi said. And she giggled as the hamster she was holding twisted out of her grip and went running for the playset. "You've definitely made the Baron's day!"

"Aw, he *looks* all happy," said Morgan. "But you know he's gonna miss you a lot."

"I'm going to miss him, too, Morgan,"

said Ash. **"I'm going to miss all of you."**

Ash held open her arms, and Morgan and Jodi and Harper and Po all gathered together for a group hug.

"You too, Theo," Ash said. "Get in here."

Theo grinned from ear to ear, happy to be included.

Ash smiled, too, even though she was crying.

Epilogue

THE POINT IN THE STORY WHERE THINGS GET WORSE . . .

Theo could hardly wait to get back to Minecraft.

He'd always loved the game. But it was *so* much better getting to share it with friends.

He'd almost gotten used to the idea that one of those friends was a digital consciousness. Life was strange!

"We're going to have to convince EK to dial back his powers, I think," Theo said as he picked up his goggles. "Otherwise our building project will be too easy!"

"You're one to talk," Jodi teased.

Theo grinned. **"Just one or two mods today,"** he said. "I promise."

He closed his eyes as he donned his headset, and when he opened them again, he was in the game. They were all there: Morgan and Jodi, Harper and Po . . .

And Ash was there, waiting for them.

"**What took you so long?**" she said.

"It's good to see you, too, Ash!" Morgan said with good-natured sarcasm.

"**you don't understand,**" she said. "**Something's wrong. Look!**"

Theo and the others gasped at the sight. There, standing atop a hill, was the Evoker King.

He had been turned to stone. *Petrified!*

"That's not possible," said Theo. "He's so powerful even without the Foundation Stone. What could do that to him?"

"I have no idea," said Ash. "But we had better find out."

"We will," said Theo.

"All of us," added Morgan. **"Together."**

MINECRAFT is a game about placing blocks and going on adventures. Build, play, and explore across infinitely generated worlds of mountains, caverns, oceans, jungles, and deserts. Defeat hordes of zombies, bake the cake of your dreams, venture to new dimensions, or build a skyscraper. What you do in Minecraft is up to you.

Nick Eliopulos is a writer who lives in Brooklyn (as many writers do). He likes to spend half his free time reading and the other half gaming. He cowrote the Adventurers Guild series with his best friend and works as a narrative designer for a small video game studio. After all these years, Endermen still give him the creeps.

Luke Flowers is an author-illustrator living in Colorado Springs with his wife and three children. He is grateful to have had the opportunity to illustrate forty-five books since 2014, when he began living his lifelong dream of illustrating children's books. Luke has also written and illustrated a best-selling book series called Moby Shinobi. When he's not illustrating in his creative cave, he enjoys performing puppetry, playing basketball, and going on adventures with his family.

Chris Hill is an illustrator living in Birmingham, England, with his wife and two daughters and has been loving it for twenty-five years! When he's not working, he loves spending time with his family and trying to tire out his dog on long walks. If there's any time left after that, he loves to go riding on his motorcycle, feeling the wind on his face while contemplating his next illustration adventure.

JOURNEY INTO THE WORLD OF

MINECRAFT™

Learn about the latest Minecraft books when you sign up for our newsletter at **ReadMinecraft.com**

Penguin
Random
House